# THE VERY NOISY HOUSE

Written by Julie Rhodes
Illustrated by Korky Paul

F

FRANCES LINCOLN
CHILDREN'S BOOKS

**For Amelia with all my love – JR**

**To Colleen Forder for getting me my first job – KP**

A big thank you to Church Cowley St James C of E Primary School,
Oxford for helping with the endpapers – KP
Front endpapers by Kara Parsons age 9 and Ragul Sivakurunathan age 9
Back endpapers by Waqas Memood age 11 and Amelia Westlake age 10

Text copyright © Julie Rhodes 2013
Illustrations copyright © Korky Paul 2013
The rights of Julie Rhodes to be identified as the author and of Korky Paul
to be identified as the illustrator of this Work have been asserted by them in accordance
with the Copyright, Designs and Patents Act, 1988.

First published in Great Britain in 2013 and in the USA in 2014 by
Frances Lincoln Children's Books, 74-77 White Lion Street,
London N1 9PF
www.franceslincoln.com

A CIP catalogue record for this book is available from the British Library

ISBN 978-1-8450-7983-3

Illustrated with watercolours

Set in Russisch Brot LT

Printed in China

3 5 7 9 8 6 4

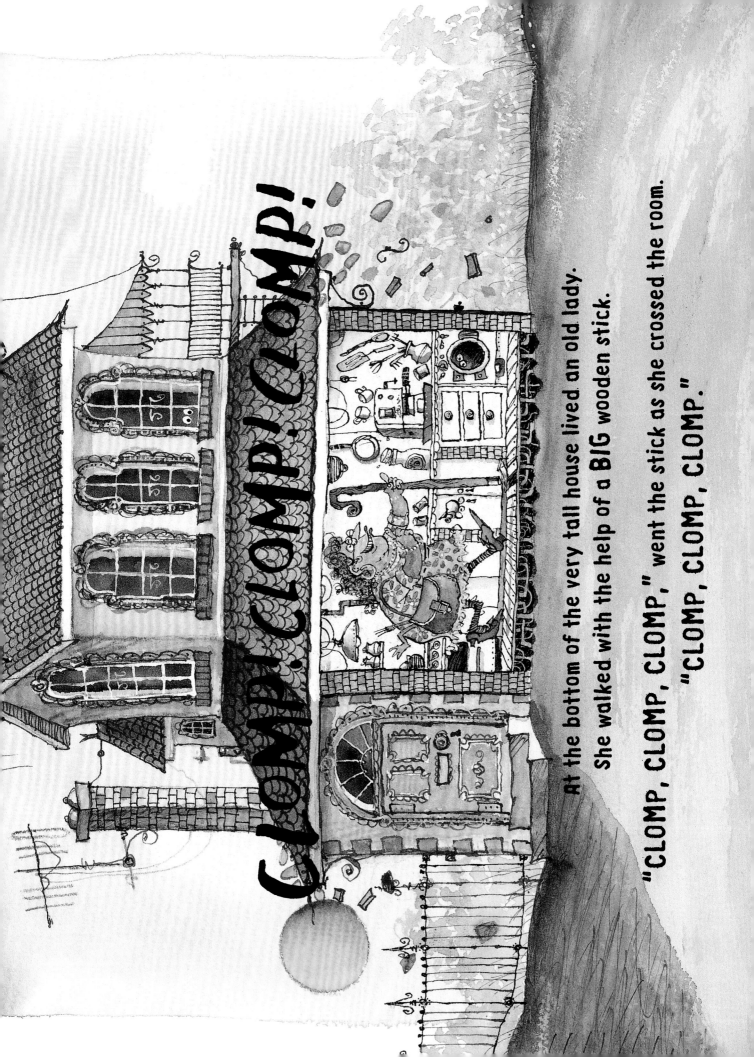

CLOMP! CLOMP! CLOMP!

At the bottom of the very tall house lived an old lady.
She walked with the help of a BIG wooden stick.

"CLOMP, CLOMP, CLOMP," went the stick as she crossed the room.
"CLOMP, CLOMP, CLOMP."

Living in the room above the old lady
was a **BIG** brown dog.
He pricked up his ears.

Is that someone knocking at the door? he thought.

He raced round the room, **BARKING**, to scare them away.
**"WOOF, WOOF, WOOF."**

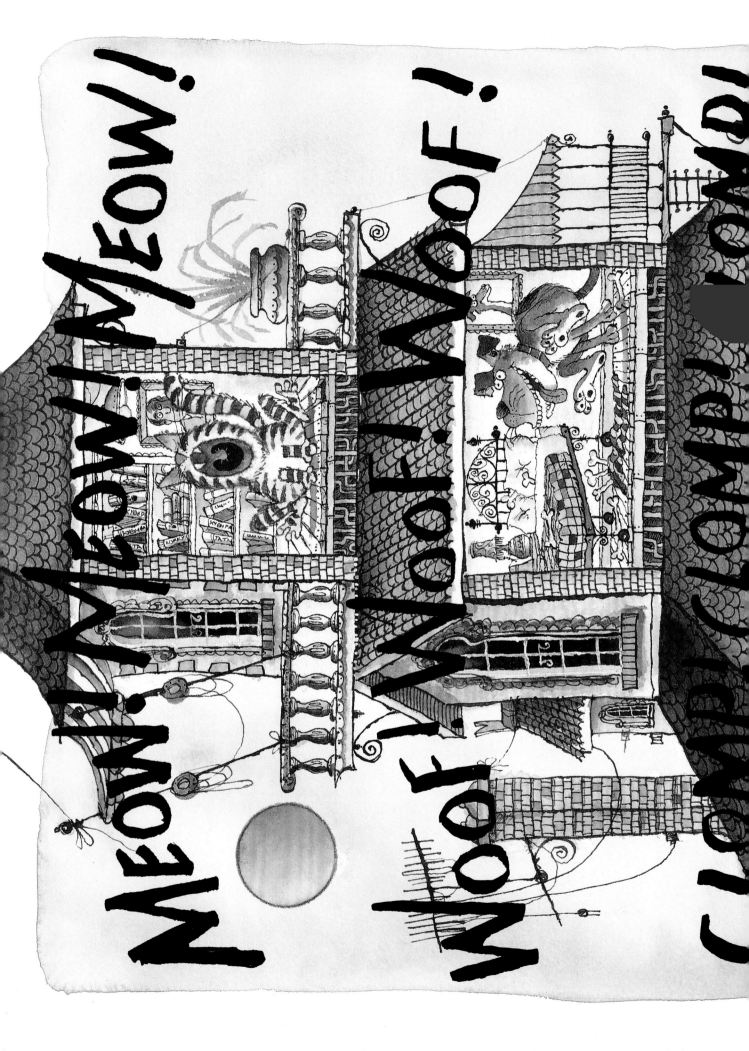

In the room above the dog,
a small ginger cat was quietly sleeping.

She opened one eye.

Is that a dog barking? It must be after me, she thought.

She began to meow LOUDLY with fright.
"MEOW, MEOW, MEOW."

# CLOMP! CLOMP! CLOMP!

In the room above the ginger cat,
a baby was PLAYING in his cot.
He heard the frightened cat MEOWING
and the noise upset him.

A tear rolled down his cheek and he began to cry.
"WHAAA, WHAAA, WHAAA."

In the attic above the baby were five roosting birds and they were disturbed by the noisy baby crying.

They FLUTTERED, squawking, into the air.
"SQUAWK, SQUAWK, SQUAWK."

SQUAWK! SQUAWK! SQUAWK!

WHAAA! WHAAA! WHAAA!

MEOW! MEOW! MEOW!

SQUAWK!SQUAWK!SQUAWK!

SQUAWK!SQUAWK!SQUAWK!

SQUAWK!SQUAWK!SQUAWK!

The baby heard the squawking birds
and didn't like the sound.

He cried even HARDER.

WHAAA!WHAAA!WHAAA!

WHAAA!WHAAA!WHAAA!

MEOW!MEOW!MEOW!

MEOW!MEOW!MEOW!

MEOW!MEOW!MEOW!

MEOW!MEOW!MEOW!

MEOW!MEOW!MEOW!

MEOW!MEOW!MEOW!

The ginger cat listened
to the baby crying
and was frightened
by the sound.

She MEOWED even more.

MEOW!MEOW!MEOW!

Woof! Woof! Woof! Woof! Woof! Woof! Woof!

CLOMP! CLOMP! CLOMP!

Woof! Woof! Woof!

Woof! Woof! Woof!

Downstairs, the barking dog heard the ginger cat meowing. He became very excited at the thought of chasing it.

He BARKED as loud as he could.

At the bottom of the tall house, the old lady was annoyed by the BARKING dog.

She BANGED her stick hard on the ceiling to try to quieten him.

At the sound of the banging, the dog BARKED louder than ever. The old lady decided to sit in her favourite chair and do some knitting to take her mind off the noise.

"CLICK, CLICK, CLICKETY-CLICK," went the knitting needles.

CLICK, CLICK, CLICK, CLICKETY CLICK

The brown dog listened to the RHYTHM of
the clicking needles and began to feel SLEEPY.
He stopped barking and settled down in his basket.

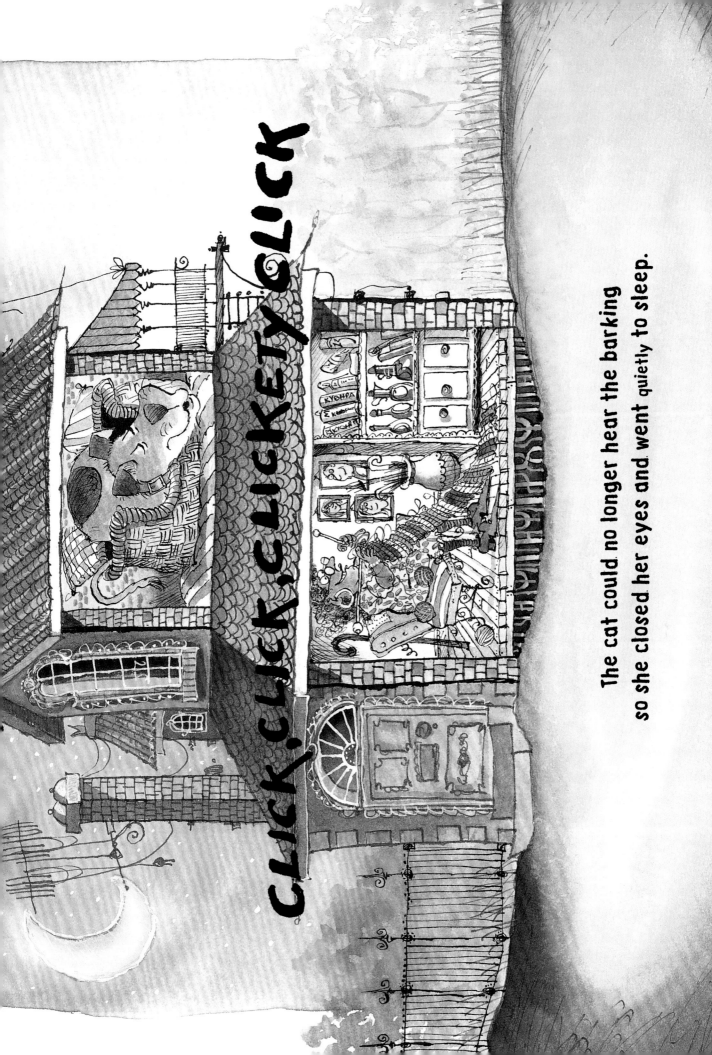

CLICK, CLICK, CLICKETY CLICK

The cat could no longer hear the barking
so she closed her eyes and went quietly to sleep.

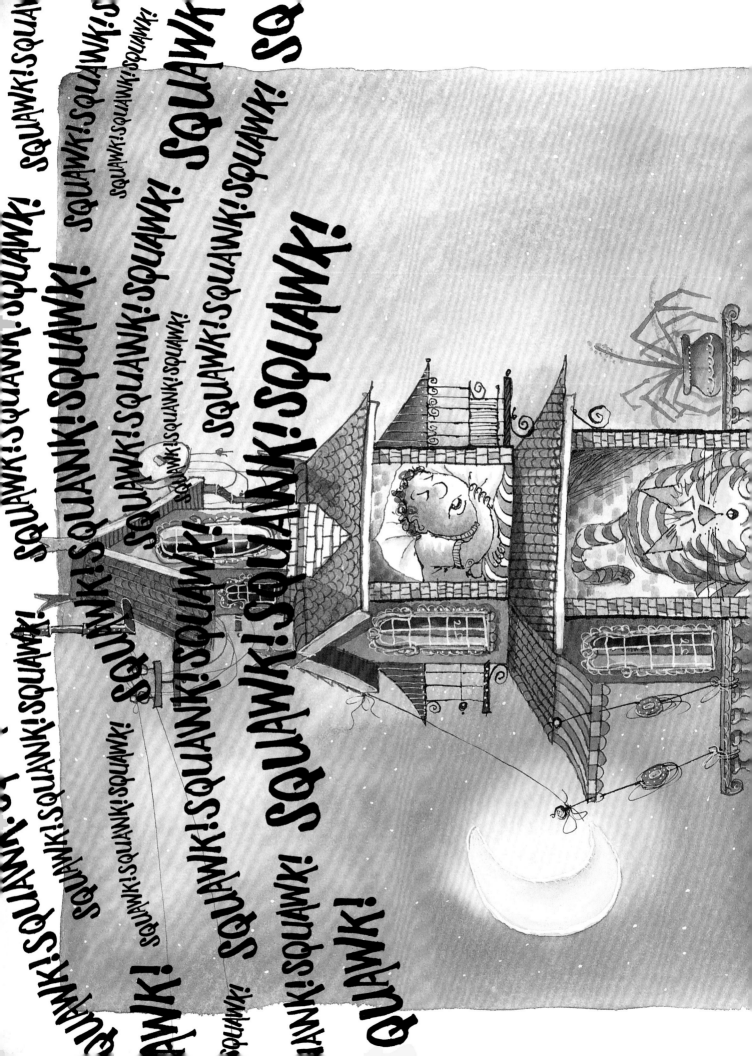

CLICK, CLICK, CLICKETY CLICK

The baby was soothed by the sound of silence
and drifted off to sleep.

The birds in the attic had some peace at last
and fluttered quietly down to roost.

"Ahh," said the old lady. "I shall make a nice cup of tea."
She got up from her chair and picked up her walking stick.

CLOMP! CLOMP! CLOMP!

"CLOMP, CLOMP, CLOMP," went the stick as she crossed the room.

"CLOMP, CLOMP, CLOMP."

The BIG, brown dog pricked up his ears....